God's Amazing World!

God's Amazing World!

Written by
Eileen Spinelli
✳ ✳ ✳
Illustrated by Mélanie Florian

ideals children's books.
Nashville, Tennessee

ISBN-13: 978-0-8249-5661-5

Published by Ideals Children's Books
An imprint of Ideals Publications
A Guideposts Company
Nashville, Tennessee
www.idealsbooks.com

Text copyright © 2014 by Eileen Spinelli
Illustrations copyright © 2014 by Mélanie Florian

Library of Congress CIP data on file

Designed by Georgina Chidlow-Rucker

Color separations by Precision Color Graphics,
    Franklin, Wisconsin
Printed and bound in China

Leo_Dec13_1

To Leo. —E.S.

Gracie was painting a picture when her little cousin Bo came to visit.

"What are you painting?" asked Bo.
"I'm painting the story of how
God made the world," she said.
"Story?" said Bo. "I love stories.
Can you tell me that story?"
"Sure," said Gracie.
"The story has **seven days.**
Like seven chapters."

"What's the first?" asked Bo.
"On the first day," said Gracie,
"God made the light and the dark."

Bo covered his eyes.

"I'm **scared** of the dark."

Gracie put her arm around Bo. "Next time you are afraid, remember this—God made the dark. Both day and night are good."

"What about the second day?" asked Bo.

"On the second day, God made the sky."

Bo jumped up. "Let's go look at the sky!"

And so they did. They lay on their backs in the grass and looked up . . . up . . . up. . . .

Bo pointed to a cloud.
"That cloud looks like
an elephant."

Gracie pointed to a different cloud.
"That one looks like a sailboat."

"God sure made a good sky," said Bo.
"Sure did," said Gracie. "Now . . .
the third day . . . follow me."

Gracie led Bo to the back garden.
The sprinkler was on. "Let's take off
our shoes and socks," said Gracie.

They took off their
shoes and socks.

They STOMPED
in the mud.

They splashed
in the sprinkler.

"Can you guess what God made on the third day?" asked Gracie.

Bo scratched his head. "Mud and water?"

"Close," said Gracie, giggling. "On the **third day**, God made the land. And the seas."

"Whew!" said Bo. "God was busy that day."

"Very busy," said Gracie. "He also told the earth to grow plants on the third day. And trees. And fruit."

"Fruit?" piped Bo. "That makes
me hungry. Let's pick peaches."
They went over to the tree by
the shed and picked peaches.

"Yum," said Bo.

"Thank you, God, for these delicious peaches," said Gracie.

Bo asked, "How about the fourth day?"

"On the fourth day, God made the sun—"
Bo waved to the sun. "Hello, Mr. Sun."
"And the moon and the stars," said Gracie.
"Where's Mr. Moon now?" asked Bo.
"I want to wave to Mr. Moon."
  "Moon is on the other side of the world now,"
said Gracie. "There may be a little boy just like
you—far, far away—waving at Mr. Moon."

"Tell me about the fifth day, Gracie."
"Birds!" Gracie said. "On the fifth day,
God made birds."

Bo began flapping his
arms like wings. "Look,
Gracie! I'm a happy,
flappy Bo-bird."

Gracie said,
"And I'm a seagull."
She and Bo flapped
and flapped until they
were all flapped out.

Then Gracie said, "And on that same day, God made creatures that swim in the sea."

Before Gracie could stop him, Bo leaped into the wading pool—with his clothes on. "Look, Gracie! I'm a happy, splashy Bo-fish."

Gracie grabbed the net they used to scoop leaves from the pool. "And I'm a fisherman." Gracie chased Bo out of the pool. They laughed so hard, Gracie got the **hiccups**.

She waited for the hiccups to go away. Then she said, "You will like the next part of the story."

Bo counted on his fingers. "The sixth day, right?"

"Right," said Gracie. "On the **sixth day**, God made animals that live on land."

Bo oinked. "I'm a piggy, Gracie. And now I'm a cow—

MOOOOO!"

Suddenly, Gracie gave a roar.
She chased after Bo again.
"And I am a lion. ROAAAAR!"

When they finally stopped racing and chasing, Gracie said, "God made something else on the sixth day."

"What?" asked Bo.

"People," said Gracie. "On the sixth day, God made people."

"Like you and me, right?" said Bo.

Gracie nodded.

"Yes. Like you and me."

Bo hugged Gracie. "I'm glad
God made you, Gracie."
Gracie hugged Bo back.
"And I'm glad God
made you, Bo."

"You said the story had seven days, Gracie. What about day seven?"

"God didn't make anything on day seven," Gracie told him. "On day seven, God rested." Bo squealed.

"God took a nap?"

Gracie smiled.

"The Bible just says God rested. And speaking of rest—" Gracie yawned. "Just thinking about God creating the world has made me sleepy."

"Me too," said Bo.